MAXWELL
FINDS A FRIEND

Written by Michael J. Pellowski
Illustrated by Anne Kennedy

Troll Associates

Library of Congress Cataloging in Publication Data

Pellowski, Michael.
    Maxwell finds a friend.

    Summary: Maxwell, a mynah bird who loves to talk,
searches among different animals for a special friend
with whom to share his house.
        [1. Mynahs—Fiction. 2. Animals—Fiction.
3. Friendship—Fiction] I. Kennedy, Anne, 1955-   ill.
II. Title.
PZ7.P3656Max   1986   [E]   85-14085
ISBN 0-8167-0586-0 (lib. bdg.)
ISBN 0-8167-0587-9 (pbk.)

10   9   8   7   6   5   4   3   2   1

MAXWELL
FINDS A FRIEND

Maxwell's house was in a tree.
It was a very nice house. And it
was very big. It had lots and
lots of rooms.

Maxwell liked living in a big,
roomy house. He liked living in
a tree. Maxwell was a bird.

6

What kind of bird was he? He
was a very special bird. He was
a bird who liked to talk.
Maxwell was a myna. Myna
birds like to talk and talk.

But Maxwell the Myna could
not talk and talk. He had no
one to talk to. Maxwell lived
alone in his big, roomy house.
Poor Maxwell.

Living alone was no fun. It was
no fun for a bird who liked to
talk. What could Maxwell do?

He tried talking to himself.
"Hello, Maxwell!" he said to
himself. "Hello, Maxwell! Hello,
Maxwell!"
But talking to himself was no
fun.

"I do not like living alone,"
Maxwell said. "I want someone
to talk to. My house is big and
roomy. I will get someone to
live with me. A roommate is
what I will get."

Maxwell thought about a
roommate. He thought and
thought. What kind of
roommate should he get? A big
roommate? A nice roommate?
"I want a special roommate,"
said Maxwell. "I want a
roommate who likes to talk."

Maxwell went out. He flew
away. He went to look for a
special roommate. Maxwell flew
here. Maxwell flew there. He
looked and looked for a
roommate.

"There is someone," cried
Maxwell. "Will that someone be
my special roommate?"
The someone was a worm.

Maxwell landed near the worm. "Hello," said the myna. "I am looking for a roommate. My name is Maxwell. What is your name?"

The worm saw the myna. He
shook from head to tail. The
worm was afraid of Maxwell.
He was too afraid to talk.
"Yipes!" cried the worm.

"Yipes?" said Maxwell. "Yipes?
What kind of name is Yipes?
What a funny name for a
worm! What a funny name for
a roommate!"

The poor worm! He was very
afraid. He could not talk.
He just shook and shook.

"I am sorry," said Maxwell.
"My roommate must be very
special. You would not be a
good roommate. Your name is
funny. And you do not talk."
Away Maxwell flew.

Maxwell flew to the lake. He saw a big buffalo. The buffalo was near the lake. Maxwell thought, "Would he be a good roommate?"

Down Maxwell went. He landed
on the buffalo's head.
"Hello," said the myna. "I live
in a nice tree. Would you like to
be my roommate?"

The buffalo did not want to live
in a tree. He did not want a
roommate. And he especially did
not want a bird on his head!
"Snort," said the buffalo.
"Snort! Snort!"

"Snort?" said Maxwell. "What kind of talk is snort? Does snort mean 'yes'? Does snort mean 'no'? What does snort mean?"

Snort meant "Go away, bird!"
The big buffalo shook his head.
"Oh, no!" cried Maxwell.
Into the lake the myna bird
went. SPLASH!

What a wet lake! What a wet
myna bird! Poor, poor Maxwell.
He did not like being wet. He
did not like the big buffalo.
"I am wet and he is not sorry,"
Maxwell said. "A buffalo is not
a good roommate for me!"

SPLASH! SPLASH! SPLASH!
A big fish was in the lake. The
fish was near Maxwell. The big
fish saw Maxwell. Maxwell saw
the fish.

"A fish for a roommate?"
thought Maxwell. "Why not?"
Maxwell said, "Hello, fish. I am
Maxwell. What is your name?"

"Glub," said the fish.
Maxwell looked at the fish.
"Glub?" Maxwell said. "What a
funny name! I am sorry, fish.
A fish named Glub would not
be a good roommate."

SPLASH! The fish went away.
Maxwell went away, too. He
splashed out of the lake.

Poor Maxwell. He was wet and lonely. He wanted a roommate to talk to. Maxwell did not like Yipes the worm. He did not like Glub the fish. He did not like the big buffalo. Where was that special someone?

Maxwell saw a tree. In the tree
was an owl.
"An owl could be a special
someone," said Maxwell. "A bird
would be a good roommate. I
will talk to the owl."

"Hi, owl," said Maxwell. "I am
Maxwell the Myna Bird. What is
your name?"
"WHO," said the owl.
"You," said Maxwell. "What is
your name?"

"WHO," cried the owl. "WHO!
WHO! WHO!"
"You," cried Maxwell. "YOU!
YOU! YOU!"
What did the owl say then?
He said, "WHO!"

The myna bird shook his head. "Sorry, owl," said Maxwell. "I cannot talk to you. Talking to an owl is not fun. You would not be a good roommate."

Maxwell went away. He went on looking. He looked and looked.

Then the myna bird saw
someone. He saw a lion. It was a
big, hungry lion. It was a lion
who liked myna birds.

Maxwell did not know the lion
was hungry. Poor, poor
Maxwell.

Maxwell went up to the hungry
lion.
"Hello, lion," said Maxwell.
"Would you like to live in a
roomy house? Would you like to
live in a tree? What do you think
of me?"

The lion did not want a roomy
house. He did not want to live in
a tree. He was hungry! The lion
wanted Maxwell. What did he
think of the myna bird?
"YUM!" said the lion.

"Yum," said Maxwell. "Yum?
What does that mean?"
Then the myna bird saw the
lion's hungry look.

Maxwell shook. He shook from
head to tail. He was very afraid.
"Oh, no!" Maxwell cried. "I
know what yum means!"

Away he flew from the hungry
lion.

Maxwell flew and flew, as quickly as he could. He did not look where he was flying.

CRASH! Maxwell flew into a
bird. It was Peter Parrot.
CRASH! Down went Maxwell
the Myna. CRASH! Down went
Peter Parrot.

"Sorry I crashed into you," said
Maxwell. "I was not looking.
I am Maxwell the Myna."
Peter said, "I am sorry, too.
I am Peter Parrot. I did not see
you. I was looking for a roomy
house to live in."

"A roomy house!" cried
Maxwell. "I have a nice, big
house with lots of rooms. Do you
like to talk? Would you like to be
my roommate?"

"I like to talk," said Peter.
"Parrots like to talk and talk.
I would like to be your
roommate."
Maxwell cried, "You are that
special someone! What a good
roommate you will be."

And what good roommates
Maxwell and Peter were!

48